Curious George®

GOES TO AN ICE CREAM SHOP

Adapted from the Curious George film series
Edited by Margret Rey and Alan J. Shalleck

1 9 8 9
Houghton Mifflin Company, Boston

Library of Congress Cataloging-in-Publication Data

Curious George goes to an ice cream shop/edited by Margret Rey and
    Alan J. Shalleck.
        p.   cm.
    "Adapted from the Curious George film series."
    Summary: Curious George makes a messy mistake while visiting a new
ice cream shop, but he redeems himself by attracting customers when
he puts together a big sundae in the window.
    ISBN 0-395-51943-8
    [1. Monkeys—Fiction. 2. Ice cream parlors—Fiction. 3. Ice
cream, ices, etc.—Fiction.] I. Rey, Margret. II. Shalleck, Alan
J. III. Curious George goes to an ice cream shop (Motion picture)
PZ7.C92166   1989   89-32363
[E]—dc20   CIP
                  AC

Printed in the United States of America

Y 10 9 8 7 6 5 4 3 2 1

George and his friend were cleaning the house.
"We've worked hard today," said the man.
"Let's treat ourselves to some ice cream."

"Look, George, there's a new ice cream place in town,"
said the man with the yellow hat. "Let's give it a try."

"We've come to try your ice cream," the man said to the owner.
"I'm glad someone has," said Mr. Herb. "Come on in."
"I just opened the place and no one knows I'm here yet."

"Well, I'll have a strawberry cone,"
said the man with the yellow hat.

Mr. Herb dipped out a scoop of strawb

George was curious. Could he s

". . . rrands to do, George," said the man.
". . . I come back. You can have
. . . 't get into trouble."

"Take your time deciding, George," said Mr. Herb.
"I'll start on a special order I have to fill."

George couldn't make up his mind.
There were so many flavors to choose from.

Mr. Herb was busy filling a bowl with ice cream.
"This is my first big order. It's for a party and it has to be just right."

Just then the phone rang. "That might be another order,"
said Mr. Herb, and he went to answer it.

The next thing you know, George had climbed onto the
counter and picked up the scoop.

He dipped it into the banana ice cream and put it
in the bowl. Then he dug into the strawberry, the
nutty walnut, the raspberry, and the chocolate.

Soon there was a mountain of ice cream in the bowl.
George was just about to put vanilla
on top of peppermint when...

"George!" Mr. Herb yelled. "That's not what my customer ordered."

"Now I have to start all over again," he said.
"Get away from here!" Mr. Herb was angry.

George was scared.

He ran over to the other counter
in front of the window.

There were jars of cherries, nuts, coconut,
whipped cream, and all kinds of sauces.
There was even a bowl of bananas.

George put some bananas in a dish.
Then he added raspberries,
chocolate chips, and whipped cream.

Mmmmm! George was getting hungry!

Suddenly, there was a tapping on the window.
George turned around.
Outside, there was a crowd watching.

"Add some nuts, George," called a boy.
"Try the sprinkles," said a girl.
"Don't forget the cherry on top."

How could George forget the cherry?

Just as George was about to taste his masterpiece,
Mr. Herb came over. He was still angry.

But before Mr. Herb could scold George,
the crowd rushed in.

"I'd like a raspberry sundae," said a man.
"And I'll have a banana split," said another.

Mr. Herb could hardly keep up. The orders kept pouring in.

Finally, everyone was served. "Thanks for all those customers,
George," Mr. Herb said. "You messed up my big
order, but you sure made up for it."

Just then, the man with the yellow hat came back.
"Have you finally decided what flavor you want, George?"
"He sure did," said Mr. Herb.

"A little of everything."